KARIUS
AND
BAKTUS

Text and illustrations by
Thorbjørn Egner

Translated by
Pat Shaw

Melody by
Christian Hartmann

CAPPELEN DAMM

HAPPY DAYS

Once upon a time there was a boy, and his name was Jens. He had teeth in his mouth, like everyone else. But in one of his teeth Jens had a cavity, and in this cavity lived two tiny fellows named Karius and Baktus. Now you might think these were strange names, but these were also strange fellows. They were so teeny weeny that you couldn't see them except through a powerful magnifying glass.

One of them had black hair and the other had red hair. They both lived on everything that was sweet and good, and they had plenty of that. They hummed and sang, and when they weren't sleeping or eating, they were hacking and hammering away in the tooth to make their house nice and big and fine.

But one day one of them thought they had done enough. "No, Karius," he said. "We've been

hammering and hacking and hammering and hacking. Now I think our house is big enough."

But Karius didn't agree. "We have to make it much bigger," he said. "You must remember, dear brother that with all the candy and caramels

we're eating nowadays, we're growing bigger and bigger with every passing hour. No – back to work, brother Baktus!"

"Very well! It's back to work."

But soon Baktus stopped working again and be-

gan to wonder. He was gazing out of the window and over at all the white teeth, and started thinking about something really fine.

"Eh Karius," he said.

"What now?" asked Karius.

6

"I was thinking. Why don't we build another house high up in that eyetooth over there? I'd much rather live there, than down here in this dump."

"Oh, you don't understand a thing, little brother. You don't understand that it's much safer to live down here. Think if that nasty old toothbrush should come!"

But then Baktus laughed, "Ho! Ho! Ho! Toothbrush! That's a laugh! Jens never brushes his teeth."

"Oh, don't be too sure," said Karius. "I remember well when he brushed them once."

"Once, yes. But that was weeks ago. Oh no.
We're quite safe here in Jens' mouth!"

Well, if you're so certain about that, you can
build wherever you like as far as I'm concerned.
But I'm going to live here," said Karius.

But Baktus stood by the window for a long time. He stared up at the white eyetooth and thought about the future, and was happy. "I'm going to live much finer than you, Karius. Just think when there are lots of us in here, and houses in all the teeth. Then, Karius, then I can sit like a king in my house and gaze out over the whole city."

"Oh you're dreaming, brother Baktus. It's not certain there'll be so many of us in here. It all depends on whether we get enough sweet food."

"Food, food, food," said Baktus. "We eat so much sweet food nowadays that we're ready to pop."

"It hasn't always been like this," said Karius. "I remember a time when the boy ate only carrots and brown bread. Phooey! Then I nearly starved to death."

"You always have to talk about something sad, Karius. You always have to talk about carrots and brown ... No, look brother! Here comes food!"

"I guess it's only brown bread."

"No, Karius, it's white bread – white bread with real syrup!" "Bravo! Bravo!"

> Hip hooray! Hooray! Hooray!
> Life is fine in every way.
> Here we have a special treat,
> All the sugar we can eat.
> Caramels both large and small
> Are the very best of all.
> And, of course, what's coming now:
> White bread thick with syrup! Wow!
> Tralalalala tralalalala
> Tralalalala lalalalala.

TWO DAYS LATER

The two tiny fellows were having a fine time. But Jens, the boy who owned the teeth, was not so happy to have them there, because teeny weeny fellows like Karius and Baktus hack out holes and ruin the teeth. And this can cause toothache. And anyone who has ever had a toothache knows there is nothing worse. You'll hear more about that in this chapter. It takes place two days later. Baktus has built a house up in the eyetooth. Now he is sitting on his balcony enjoying himself, while Karius is hacking and hammering away down in the old house.

"Hello Karius, are you down there?"

"You can hear that I'm working, can't you?"

"What are you doing?"

"I'm making an underground tunnel from my tooth over to your tooth."

"That's a good idea!" said Baktus.

13

"How are you getting along up there?" asked Karius.

"I'm fine. Now I'm sitting and enjoying the view. Only white peaks as far as I can see."

"But brother, what's that whining sound?"

"Shhhh! listen," said Baktus.

"I HAVE SUCH A TERRIBLE TOOTH-ACHE!"

"Oh pooh! it's only Jens who's whining," said Baktus.

"Could you hear what he said?" asked his brother.

"He said: 'I have such a terrible toothache!'" mimicked Baktus. And then they both laughed.

"Hahaha!"

16

"I think Jens is a regular crybaby," said Baktus.

"I'm going to tease him a little," said Karius eagerly. "I'm going to hammer in a spot where I know it hurts. Listen!" And then he hammered three times in a spot deep, deep down inside.

"OW! OW! OW!"

"Did you hear anything?" he asked.

"He said: 'OW! OW! OW!'" said Baktus, and they laughed so hard their tummies shook."

"Do it again, Karius!"

And Karius did it again.

(Dunk, dunk!)

"I HAVE SUCH A TERRIBLE TOOTH-ACHE!"

"Hahahahahaha," laughed both tiny fellows.

"YOU MUST BRUSH YOUR TEETH, JENS!"

Karius looked up at his brother in dismay.

"Who was that?" he asked.

"That was Jens' mother," said Baktus.

"What did she say?"

"She said: 'You must brush your teeth, Jens'."

"Oh, woe is us, Baktus. Think if he comes with that nasty toothbrush? What shall we do?"

"We'll trick him into not brushing his teeth," said Baktus. "We'll shout at him and tell him not to do as his mother says. We'll shout at the same time. One two three:

Don't do as your mother says, Jens!

Don't do as your mother says!"

"He's doing it anyway!" cried Baktus. "I can hear him filling a glass with water! And here comes the toothbrush! Help, Karius! Help!"

"Hurry up, Baktus! Jump down here with me! It's safer down here than up there!"

And Baktus dived down from his house and crawled in with Karius. And just in time. He had barely squeezed his pudgy little bottom inside when the terrible toothbrush came swoosing past. And water and foam poured all the way in to the tiny fellows.

"Phooey! Phooey! Ugh – I'm nearly choking

from this nasty toothpaste!" said Karius, spitting
and coughing.

"And listen to all the noise it's making!" said
Baktus. "Phooey! Phooey!"

"There, he stopped at last."

"Do you think we can sneak out now?" asked
Baktus.

"Careful, careful," said Karius, and they ope-
ned the door a crack.

"Oh what a sorrowful sight," said Baktus.

"What's the matter?" asked Karius.
"Everything's gone. Not one bit of food left."
"Not even a crumb left."

There is nothing left to eat.
Everything that's nice and sweet
Mean old toothbrush swept away
All the food is gone today.
There is not a single bite
Not a caramel in sight.
No more bread or syrup too.
What on earth are we to do?

AT THE DENTIST'S

After Jens had brushed his teeth he felt a little better. But it was not much better because the cavities were still there. And early the next morning, the tiny fellows started hammering again.

It was then that Jens' mother had a bright idea. And you will learn all about it in the third chapter, which takes place at the dentist's.

"Why are you so angry, dear brother?"

"I'm hungry," said Karius.

"Something sweet will be coming soon," said Baktus.

"It doesn't look like it."

"Perhaps we could try to talk to Jens."

"Talk! talk!" said Karius. "He doesn't listen to us any longer."

"If we shout at the same time, he might listen," said Baktus.

"What'll we shout?" asked his brother.

"Let's shout: We want white bread!"

"Very well, we can try," said Karius. And then they both shouted:

"We want white bread!
We want white bread!"

"OPEN WIDE!"

"Did you hear something?" asked Karius.

"I heard a man talking," said Baktus in surprise.

"What did he say?"

"He said: Open wide!"

"That's funny," said Karius.

"Perhaps it was the Baker who said 'Open wide'," said Baktus happily. "Perhaps it helped to shout! Look, now he's opening his mouth."

"I hope it has syrup on it," said Karius.

They waited a while but no food appeared. Then Baktus became impatient. "What on earth! How long is he going to open wide before something comes?" he asked.

"Oh dear! Look how light it is in here. It's as if the whole sun is shining in," said Karius.

"What do you think that is?" asked Baktus.

"I don't know," said Karius. "I'll give you a shove and then you can climb up and have a look."

Baktus climbed up on his shoulders and peeked over the edge.

"Can you see anything?" asked Karius.

"Oh woe is me! What can I see? I can see a big lamp just outside his mouth. It's ten times bigger than the sun!"

"Oh dear! Oh dear! Can you see anything else?"

"I can see a man in a white jacket!"

"Oh woe is me! Then it's the dentist!"

"Are dentists dangerous?"

"Dentists? Oh yes. They're the most dangerous of all. They fill our cavities!"

"Oh Karius, I'm afraid!"

"What's that buzzing sound?" asked Karius.

"There's something big and ugly and shiny that's buzzing and whirring around," said Baktus.

"Oh dear! Oh dear! Then it's a drill!"

"It's coming closer and closer!" shouted Baktus.

"What'll we do? Help! It's coming over here!"

"We must run away! Come, Baktus! Come!"

Baktus jumped down and both tiny fellows

ran all the way to the back of Jens' mouth.

They stood behind the innermost molar and watched in horror at what was happening. And they became angrier and angrier.

"Look Karius, now he's drilling in our cavities!"

"Oh, I'm so mad!"

"Shall we run over and bite the drill?" saked
Baktus

"We can't do that, it's too hard," said Karius.

"We can bite his finger," said Baktus.

"That won't help," said Karius.

"We can jump up inside his mouth and hammer on his teeth," shouted Baktus. He was fuming.

"No Baktus, it's impossible to fight against dentists."

"I wish there wasn't a single dentist in the whole wide world! Look! Now he's spouting water in our cavities."

"Ugh, what a mess!" said Karius.

"Look Karius, now he's filling my nice house in the eyetooth. Oh! Oh! Oh! Now I'm going to run over and bite him!"

"Stop, Baktus! He'll just rinse you out!"

"Look, now he's filling your house too," shouted Baktus. And Karius was so furious he was ready to pop. "Stop that! Hey there, Dentist! Stop that!"

"He's not listening," said Baktus.

"He doesn't want to listen," said Karius.

"And now it's too late," said Baktus. "Now he has finished. That was my fine house with a view

33

and everything. Now it's all gone."

"And this was my big cavity. That's gone too," said Karius.

"Not even a teeny-weeny cavity left," said Baktus.

> Where are we to sleep tonight?
> All the teeth are smooth and white.
> I'm so mad! So mad! So mad!
> evermore will I be glad.
> But there's nothing we can do,
> We're too small and helpless too.
> We're so tired – but we know
> There's no place for us to go.

FINAL CHAPTER

IN THE EVENING

J ens went home from the dentist's. He was hap--
py because he no longer had any cavities or
toothache. But how were Karius and Baktus getting

on? Not very well. and in the final chapter we shall find out what happened to them in the end.

"These are bad times, Baktus!"

"Yes, dear brother, bad times."

"Nothing sweet to eat and no place to live."

"Nothing sweet to eat and no place to live."

"Phooey!" said Karius.

"Phooey!" said Baktus.

– – –

"Perhaps we should try to sleep here in this corner tonight."

"I'm so hungry I can't sleep," said Karius.

"No," said Baktus. "But look, brother, Jens is opening his mouth! Perhaps something good is coming."

"I doubt if it's anything good."

"Give me a shove brother, and I'll climb up and have a look," said Baktus.

And Karius shoved and Baktus peeked over the edge.

"Can you see anything?"

"I see - I see! Oh what a sorry sight!"

"What do you see?" asked Karius.

"The brush! That toothbrush again!"

Baktus scrambled down as fast as he could.

"What'll we do?"

"Not a cavity to crawl into," said Karius.

"Not a cavity to hide in," said Baktus.

"Jens! Jens! Mercy! Mercy!" shouted both the tiny fellows. And Karius said: "We'll never bother you again! We'll never bother you again, I say!"

"We must hide, Karius!"

"Yes but, where – where?"

At the same moment the toothbrush came swooshing along so the foam flowed.

"Help! Help! The toothbrush is taking me!" shouted Baktus.

"Hold on tight, Baktus!"

"I can't! Help! Help!"

"Let go, you nasty brush!"

"Help!"

But it didn't help. They no longer had any cavities to hide in, and so they were brushed out of the mouth along with toothpaste and water and foam. They fell down through the sink and down through the drainpipe and far out on the deep blue sea. And there they are, sailing about, waiting

for another cavity to creep into.

Now you might feel a little sorry for Karius and Baktus. But there was someone who was happy that everything turned out the way it did. And that was the boy who owned the teeth. That was Jens.

THE HAPPY MELODY

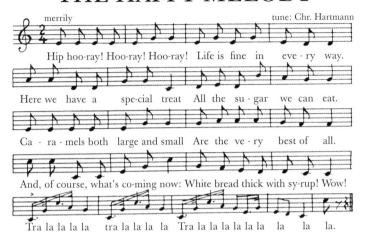

Hip hoo-ray! Hoo-ray! Hoo-ray! Life is fine in eve - ry way.

Here we have a spe-cial treat All the su - gar we can eat.

Ca - ra - mels both large and small Are the ve - ry best of all.

And, of course, what's co-ming now: White bread thick with sy-rup! Wow!

Tra la la la la tra la la la la la Tra la la la la la la la la la.

THE SAD MELODY

Where are we to sleep to - night? All the teeth are

smooth and white. I'm so mad! So mad! So mad! Ne - ver - more will

I be glad. But there's no-thing we can do, We're too small and

help-less too. We're so ti - red but we know. There's no place for

us to go.